Can't Yeti Enough

SABRINA CROSS

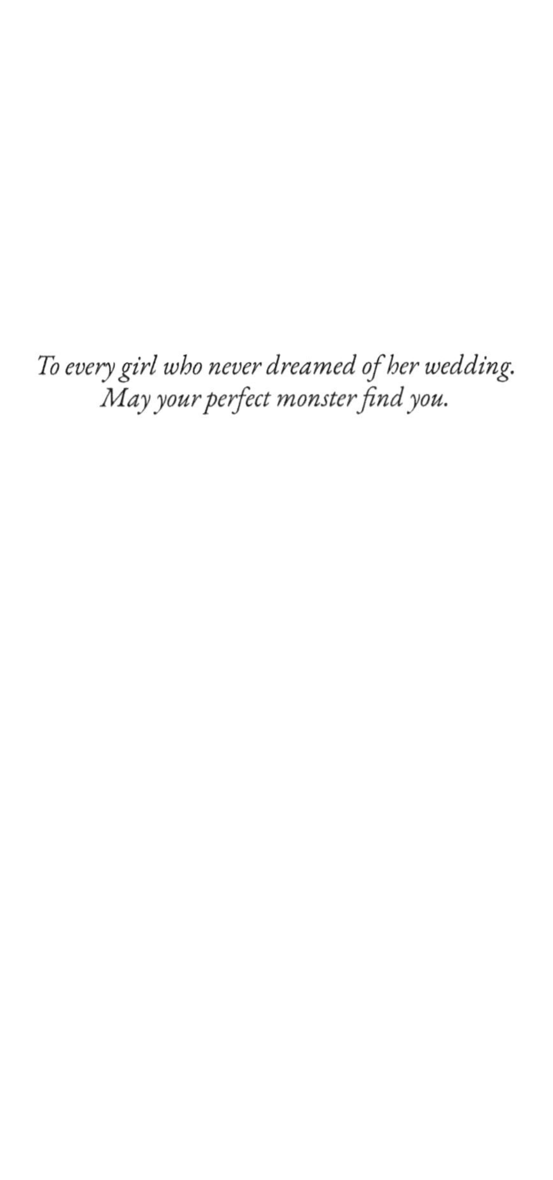

To every girl who never dreamed of her wedding.
May your perfect monster find you.

Author's Note

This is a monster romance. Humans will be getting it on with non-human entities. Don't worry, everyone is gleefully consenting.

If you read the last three sentences and think that's not for you, that's okay. There is still time to put this book down and walk away. No one will blame you. It's the sane thing to do.

But if you're going to stick around please be aware of the following:

Can't Yeti Enough is a story of snowed-in, insta-love with an adorable himbo yeti. It contains themes of child abandonment, verbally crappy boyfriends, light dub-con, and graphic sex with a non-human entity.

If you feel I am missing anything please reach out to me at authorsabrinacross@gmail.com and let me

know. A complete list can be found at www.sabri-
nacross.com

Chapter One

"Will you marry me, Haley?" I stared down at my boyfriend of two years in absolute horror. Most little girls grow up dreaming of hearing those words. I was never one of them.

The other hikers standing around the peak of Mount Bay stopped to stare at my idiot boyfriend down on one knee, holding up the ugliest ring I had ever seen. Of course, he chose to do it there, of all places. Despite knowing I never wanted to get married, I have no intention of having children, and there was no way in hell I was changing my name to Haley Anne Buttson.

"Hay-Hay, I kind of need an answer here." Dylan sounded nervous and a little annoyed. I don't know what he expected. I would fall to my knees in gratitude?

Fuck. That.

"No." People around us gasped and giggled. I didn't pay them any mind. Let them enjoy the show Dylan decided to put on for their benefit. It certainly wasn't for mine.

If it had been for me, he wouldn't have done it at all and he certainly wouldn't have chosen that moment in that place to do it. No, it was a show and a manipulation. Dylan had chosen somewhere I couldn't easily walk away from him. He'd chosen a time when I was high on success, hoping it would, I don't know, change my mind from a lifetime of being against marriage.

Hiking Mount Bay had been a goal of mine for years. I'd worked hard to get fit enough to make it to the peak of the tallest mountain in the state and he decided now, the first time I'd ever managed to do so, to get down on one knee in the snow and make my moment about him.

I repeat: Fuck that.

Dylan surged to his feet, ring box snapping closed in his fisted hand. His face was red and rage burned in his blue eyes. Well, fuck him. He was the one who put himself in that position.

"What do you mean no?" He demanded, spittle flying from his lips. Gross.

"I mean no. I told you, I don't want to get married." I was my parents' only child, despite having more step-and half siblings than I could count. My father was on his third marriage, my mother was about to wed her fifth husband. Marriage didn't mean anything to me except a piece of paper and a way to make it legally difficult to break up with someone. I didn't have a religious or moral reason to do it, so why would I ever allow myself to be trapped?

"I didn't think you were serious!" Dylan raised his hands in frustration and it took a lot not to flinch. He'd never been abusive, but I'd also never seen him so angry before. "Do you know how much this ring cost? What am I supposed to tell my family? Our friends? They all expect us to be engaged when we reach the bottom!"

"Sounds like a you problem." Red touched the edges of my vision. I couldn't believe he would tell everyone he was doing this. I also couldn't believe not one person told him this was a terrible idea.

So much for our friends. They clearly didn't know a thing about me if no one stopped him from pulling this bullshit.

"Haley, you can't be serious." His voice was taking on a whine that had me gritting my teeth. There was nothing I hated more than whining. Which was yet another reason I didn't want kids of my own.

"I'm completely serious. I don't know how you expected this to go but I've been very clear for the last two years. I have zero interest in marriage." I gripped my bag straps to keep from gripping his shoulders and shaking some sense into him.

"When are you going to grow up and get over it? Stop letting some childhood trauma ruin your life." Dylan spat the words and I reeled back on my heels.

"I think the only thing I've done to ruin my life is waste so much of it with you." I turned and started walking the path back down the hill. I knew I should wait for the rest of the crew we climbed up with but I was not going to stand there and let him insult and injure me.

The tears started falling shortly after I entered the trees. I wasn't sad. I was pissed. How fucking dare he? How dare he ignore everything I'd ever said? How dare he take my achieving moment and turn it into a shitshow about him? The goddamn audacity of it!

I wasn't paying much attention as I carefully made my way down the mountain. I was putting in just enough focus as it took to not fall down on the steep trail. I wanted to put as much distance between Dylan and I as possible. The temptation to shove him down the mountain was too strong, and I was terrible at resisting temptation. Unfortunately, Dylan had been hiking his entire life, and I'd only been doing it for the last year or so. It wouldn't take him much effort at all to overtake me on the path.

Hopefully, he had the sense to either take it slow or detour off onto the other path meant for experienced hikers. It was quicker and I would risk running into him at the bottom. On that note, I pulled my phone out of the side pocket on my pack to start making calls for someone to pick me up. Dylan and I had driven out together and damn if I'd spend forty-five minutes in the car with him to get back to town.

Of course, there was no service so high up. I sighed and put my phone back. While I was focused on my phone, my foot slipped on some loose rocks and I went down. I slipped into near splits before landing solidly on my ass.

"Well, at least it's padded." I muttered as I took inventory of my situation. It was cold and getting colder. There was a storm supposed to be hitting the area late that night, and I could already feel it in the breeze. Gently pushing to my feet, I winced as my ankle buckled under my weight. It was painful, but I could stand on it. It wasn't like I had a choice. I had to make it down the mountain before nightfall. I had no phone service, and I'd rather freeze to death than ever ask Dylan the Douche for help.

"Which is what you're going to have to do if you don't get moving." I told myself, forcing one foot in front of the other. It had been a four-and-a-half hour hike up the mountain and with my ankle, it would take me much longer to get back down.

I kept my eye on the sides of the path, looking for something I could use as a walking stick. The longer I kept walking on the steep decline, the more my ankle hurt. I had only been walking for about an hour before the snow, that was supposed to hit after midnight, started floating down.

"Well, fuck."

Chapter Two

I was fucked. I was well and truly fucked.

What had started as some light flurries quickly turned into a wet, heavy snow. My feet were sticking with every step which killed my ankle. I guessed Dylan really had taken the experienced path along with the other hikers because I hadn't seen anyone since I had left them at the top of the mountain.

I was in pain, gasping for air, and every part of me was freezing, despite the energy I was exerting to keep putting one foot in front of the other. I had to do something, and fast, or I was going to die on that damn mountain.

There was still no service on my phone. Not that I'd really expected any. We'd lost it about an hour into our hike. We had a handheld radio, but that had been in Dylan's pack. I was completely alone.

I looked around, wondering if there was any-where I could take shelter. Everyone said not to go into the caves on Mount Bay lest you meet the beast of the mountain. But I was cold, tired, in pain, and honestly wouldn't even care if something ate me.

At least then I'd stop shivering.

A flash of light caught my eye. It was distant, through the trees. I couldn't see the source of it. Maybe it was the other group. I wasn't sure where the other path went and how close it might run to mine at times.

"Don't go off the path, Hay." My dad's voice in my head when I'd told him about my hiking challenge. "Bad things happen on that mountain."

Still, there was nothing but snow up and down my path and there was definitely a flicker of light just at the edge of my vision, straight through the woods. If I could reach the other group of hikers, maybe one of them would have a radio. I really wasn't sure if I was going to be able to make it down the mountain with my ankle in that condition, especially not trudging through snow. The snow patrol would be out and they could rescue me. I was sure of it.

I just needed a radio or cell service.

With one last glance down the path, I stepped off and started forging my own toward the flickering light.

My heart was racing as I moved under the trees. Though I found some relief to my aching ankle as the canopy kept the worst of the snow out. It was darker under the trees and I debated pulling my bag off and digging out my flashlight. The light ahead of me didn't seem far away and I didn't want to slow down or stop. I was terrified I would lose momentum and they'd find my body sometime in the spring.

That was, if the monster of the mountain or the other wild animals didn't tear me apart for food first.

"Morbid much?" I asked myself, trying to keep me going. "You're not going to die out here, Haley. Yes, it's cold and if you don't find the other path, you're definitely lost but you're not going to die. You're supposed to meet up with Emma tonight and she'll send the national guard if you don't show up.

Emma was my half-sister on my father's side. She was a lot of years younger than me, but we were pretty close for kids who only saw each other a couple times a year growing up. Emma was twenty-three to my thirty-one, we'd shared a bedroom on my weekend visits to my dad's house. She was one of three half-siblings I had between both parents. I also had a string of step-siblings. Most of which I kept in contact with after our parents divorced, much to my bio parent's consternation.

When they divorced, they wanted clean breaks. Which explained my less than regular visitations with my father growing up. Why step-dad two dropped as assistant coach of my soccer team in middle school. Why step-mom three decided not to take me shopping for my prom dress after she and Dad split. I'd gone dress shopping with her daughter, who was a year younger than me.

Thinking about my family was always complicated. I'd learned to love my parents for who they were and to stop expecting more from them than what they were capable of giving. It'd taken a lot of time and therapy but I was in a good place with them. Which is why Dylan's childhood trauma comment filled me with so much rage. I didn't have childhood trauma anymore. I had thousands of dollars in therapy visits that took care of that. I just didn't see the point of participating in an antiquated ritual that only really benefited the man.

The light was closer now. I could see it just through the trees. Something about it wasn't right. I'd been heading toward what I had assumed was a flashlight, but the light was flickering and caused the shadows to dance weirdly through the trees.

"Oh, no." That definitely wasn't a flashlight. I was looking at someone's fire. And anyone dumb enough to be building a fire on a night like this instead of finding shelter was probably someone I didn't want to run into while alone and unarmed in the woods.

I turned around quickly and started heading back to my own path, away from whoever was camping out illegally in the mountains. I moved quickly while being as quiet as I possibly could. A weird grumble came from behind me. Without looking over my shoulder, I started running. The hell with my ankle, I needed out of there and fast.

I only made it a short distance before I caught my bad foot in a tree root and went down. My head slammed against the base of the tree along the way.

My last thought as things went dark: at least I would never have to see Dylan again.

Chapter Three

It was the heat that woke me. The last thing I remembered was running through the woods away from an illegal campsite. The throbbing in my head and face suggested I hit it on something. None of that explained why I was so warm.

I cracked my eyelids and winced at the flickering firelight. I struggled to sit up, a pile of fur pelts acted as blankets. They weighed a lot and made the task difficult. The room I was in was bare, rough stone walls and ceiling, a cave of some kind.

I had pushed myself up into a sitting position when the room went dark, the edges of my vision blurring. My head was in agony. Every part of me wanted to lie back down and go to sleep. That was a very dangerous idea.

Especially as I took inventory of myself and realized my backpack, boots, coat, socks, and pants were all missing. I wouldn't have been too worried about my pack and boots, given I was lying in a makeshift bed. The lack of pants worried me. A lot.

I slid out from under the pelts and got to my

feet, having to brace my hand against the cold stone wall for a moment as the room went dark again. I reached up and pressed a hand against my throbbing head. The pain was blinding.

My hair was matted with what I could only assume was dried blood. The side of my head and part of my face throbbed and felt like it was on fire. I leaned against the wall and bent over, trying to catch my breath and regain my balance.

I slowly straightened up and leaned back against the wall for balance. Across the small cavern there is a brilliant fire. Laid out or hanging on boulders nearby are all of my missing things. It was both comforting and terrifying. I was glad my clothes weren't missing. Still, someone had undressed me down to my underwear before tucking me into bed.

Looking around, I tried to find the way out. There were two openings, both gaping maws of darkness. I couldn't see any light down either direction. I was trapped.

Fuck.

"Deep breath, Hay. Get your clothes on, find your pack, check for cell service." Although, I highly doubted I had any cell service in a fucking cave somewhere halfway up a mountain.

I pushed away from the wall and waited for the room to settle again before making my way slowly, painfully, across the frigid stone floor to where my clothes were. I wanted to be ready for when whoever undressed me came back. There was no way I was facing my rescuer/kidnapper in nothing but my underwear and t-shirt.

The fire was so warm against my skin, blazing high. The smoke coiled and spun upward. It should have been suffocating but when I looked up there was a small ventilation hole in the ceiling of the cave. It wasn't very large and I could see snow falling through and melting under the heat of the fire.

Okay, so I wasn't very deep into the caves if there was sky above me. And it was still snowing. Hopefully that meant I hadn't been out long. Maybe the snow patrol was already looking for me. Maybe if I could find my way out of the cave, I could be rescued and taken to safety quickly.

Probably the safety of a hospital, if my head was any indication of the shape I was in. I looked down at my purple and swollen ankle. I could walk on it, so it wasn't broken. I'd definitely done some damage.

Fuck Dylan. Fuck him into oblivion for talking me into hiking and then abandoning me on a mountain. Once I got down, I was never going near a mountain again.

I made it across the large cave and grabbed my socks. They were still a little damp, but warm from the fire. I could live with it. I leaned back against the boulder holding my pants and slowly, painfully, put them on.

A noise down one of the tunnels caught my attention. There was a scuffling, dragging sound. Someone was coming and dragging their feet. I didn't know if I had time to finish getting dressed. I didn't know how long that tunnel was or how soon they would be there.

Quickly, I tugged my pants and coat off of the rocks and balled them up in my arms. I would at least have enough to not freeze to death. I shoved my feet in my unlaced hiking boots and slid behind the boulder as quietly as I could.

From my spot behind the large rock, I couldn't see the tunnel opening, but I could see the majority of the cave. The fire, the makeshift bed on the floor. There was a collection of odds and ends piled high in a corner. Pots, dishware, backpacks, fabrics.

My heart started racing. That was some serial killer clutter if I ever fucking saw some. Oh god, I was going to die in a cave.

No. The fuck I was.

I tightened my grip on my clothes and dug my toes into my boots, ready to make a run for it just as soon as the person passed by my hiding place. One of those tunnels would lead to the outside and either was better than whatever that psycho had in mind for me.

The footsteps shuffled to a stop just on the other side of the boulder. There was a grunt and a snuffle. Oh fuck. What if it wasn't a person at all? What if an animal made its way into the cave to get out of the snow?

I wasn't sure which scared me more. A trapped animal or a possible psycho killer. I just knew I needed to get the fuck out of there. I didn't care if I was half naked, my head was killing me, or that I was already freezing. I was going to make my escape.

That was the moment the beast stepped forward.

It was huge. At first I thought, bear. Except, it was white and there sure as fuck weren't any polar bears in the Colorado mountains. It stood on two legs, a giant, looming presence in the cave. Its white fur was dingy and dirty around its tree-trunk legs.

Its torso was broad and long, excessively long arms held a huge bundle of logs. Hair continued over its entire body, over its neck and torso and arms. Its hands were black and leathery like a dog's nose.

I slapped my hand over my mouth to keep the sound from escaping. It was a monster. I was trapped in a cave with a monster.

I watched silently as it dropped the logs and made its way to the bed.

"Human?" The voice was a growl, the word barely comprehensible. "Human? Where at?"

It bent over to pull back the furs and I saw its face. Large black eyes, an apeish nose, wide pink mouth. I was looking at a fucking albino sasquatch.

Okay. Okay.

Monsters were real, and I was trapped in a cave with one.

Cool.

Cool, cool, cool, cool, cool.

I could handle this.

Nope, I could not handle it.

I shifted, preparing to dart from behind the boulder and out the tunnel opening when it whirled around.

"Human!" Its face lit up, "There you at."

Oh, fuck.

It had found me.

Chapter Four

I was locked in a cave with a monster and it was watching me with such glee on its face I knew I was going to be its next meal. There was no way I was giving up without a fight.

The thing might be nearly eight feet tall and build like a freight train, but I was short and fast and there was a chance I could outrun it. How quick could something so big be?

With a squeak, I dodged out from behind the boulder and headed for the cave opening. Left or right? Left. I took off out the entrance and down the pitch black tunnel. The air was frigid, and I hoped that meant I was heading in the right direction. Except it didn't stay frigid for long. Soon it was getting humid and I could hear running water.

A hot spring? I hadn't realized Mount Bay had any hot springs. Still, if I could find it and follow the water, maybe it would lead me out of the cave. I could hear the monster behind me, roaring as it gave chase.

Light filtered in ahead. It was bleak, but it was

something. I tripped out of my shoes and sprinted in my socks toward the end of the tunnel.

"Human, no!" The beast yelled as I reached the end of the tunnel. I ignored it, pressing forward.

I barely had a moment to see the light filtering in through multiple holes in the cave ceiling before I went off the edge of a cliff.

My scream barely had a chance to escape before I splashed into the pool of water. My clothes went flying and landed in the water around me. Shit.

"Human want bath?" The monster peered down at me from the edge of the pool, a solid six feet above me. It looked more confused than angry. "Okay, we bath."

Without warning, the beast jumped off the edge and into the pool, cannon-balling into the water, sending it splashing over my head. The pool was deep enough I couldn't touch the bottom and I struggled to stay above water. The edges were deep on all sides and there was nothing for me to hold onto.

I was still coughing and sputtering when the monster emerged beside me, scooping me up into its furry arms. I struggled against it, to escape.

"Shhh, shhh, okay." A large hand began patting me on my head. The monster was...soothing me? I stopped fighting to stare up at it. Confused. Was it hoping to lull me into compliance before eating me? "Good. Better now?"

It was clearly waiting for some sort of response from me. I nodded, forcing myself to relax. To wait and see what it did next.

"Clothes wet again." He reached out and

grabbed my floating jacket and pants, throwing them over the ledge to the cliff I fell from.

"Yeah," I said dumbly. The monster grinned at me, revealing many blunt off-white teeth. "Clothes are wet again. They'll dry."

"By fire. Fire dry clothes." The monster started tugging at my shirt. I slapped its hands away. "Shirt wet." It said.

"Yeah, well, I'm not taking it off." I crossed my arms, bringing them up against its broad chest.

"Wet clothes make human sick." The monster shrugged. "Dumb human."

I didn't even know how to respond to that. I was being called dumb by a monster that I would have sworn didn't exist. I was pretty sure I was going insane. It was the most logical explanation.

Except, I didn't feel crazy, and the monster felt very, very real. Real and solid. Its heart beat strong and hard against my arms, where they rested against his chest. Its breath was warm on my face, warmer than the hot spring we stood in. My legs instinctually wrapped around it and I yelped.

Okay, him. It was definitely a him. A very large and aroused him.

I shoved away, battling against his grip on me. He went back to patting my head and shushing me. Slowly, I allowed him to soothe me back down.

Logically, he hadn't done anything threatening. He wasn't trying to get my clothes off. He wasn't even grinding against me. He had a cock. The cock was hard. Biology. That was all it was.

"Good human." He ran his hand down my hair and cupped my face. He used his grip to turn my head this way and that. "Pretty human."

"Thank you." The response was automatic and insane. "Can we get out of here?"

"No run?" He glared at me but made his way toward the ledge we'd come over. "Not safe."

"I won't run." I was pretty sure I could make it back to the cavern with the fire and out the other tunnel that certainly led outside. But I was soaking wet, half-naked, and the snow was still falling. It would be suicide to go outside like this.

So I would wait. Bide my time until I had a chance to escape. Hopefully, with my pants and coat back on.

"Good human." The monster grinned a giant, toothy grin before grabbing me around the waist and throwing me up over the ledge.

Chapter Five

"Stay." The creature set me on a rock near the fire before going about laying my wet clothes out to dry. He'd insisted on carrying me down the tunnel, my bundle of dripping clothing in my arms.

I kicked off my boots and pulled off my soaked socks before putting my feet as close to the fire as I dared. My ankle was swollen but not too terribly. And the pain was minimal. It was the least of my concerns as the cold of the cave started settling in. I had an emergency blanket in my pack, which I could see by the entrance to the cave. I couldn't bear the thought of walking barefoot across the cave. I'd certainly have frostbite before I made it that far.

Shivers wracked my body, and I slid closer to the fire. At my movement, the creature spun on me with a growl.

"Stay!"

Fear was a distant emotion compared to the cold seeping into my bones. My reckless brain figured death by a snow beast would probably be quicker and less painful than freezing to death.

"Not happening." I scooted closer to the fire, feeling the warmth hit me in weak waves. "Unless you want me to freeze to death."

The creature grumbled under his breath but didn't stop me when I slid off of the rock and onto the cave floor next to the waning flames. I crouched on the ground as close to the fire as I could get, my body shook with cold.

I curled up, my arms around my icy legs, my toes nearly touched the rock ring making up the fire pit. I had never been so cold in my life, even with the fire. Something soft and warm settled over my shoulders. I glanced up as the creature wrapped me in a coat.

It wasn't mine. It had likely belonged to a large man. There was a slightly stale smell to it.

Previous victim. My brain whispered. I wondered how true that was.

"Thanks," I muttered, sliding my arms into the sleeves and wrapping it around my legs as much as I could.

"Now stay." He glared down at me and I nodded, not wanting to anger him.

"Where would I go?" I asked, as much to him as myself.

"Ran before," his glare was pointed.

I felt kind of sheepish about that. And not just because my attempt at escape had ended so terribly.

"Whose coat is this?" I asked. I wondered if he'd tell me. If I could believe the answer.

"Human. Gone now." He shrugged his giant shoulders, the movement a little sad. "Humans come, humans go. Krogan stay here."

"Krogan," I asked. "Is that your name?"

The creature nodded and beat a fist against his chest. "Me Krogan."

"I'm Haley," I gave Krogan a tentative smile. Maybe he wouldn't eat me if we became friends.

"Hay-lee" He repeated with a wide grin that showed many, many blunt ivory teeth. I tried to hide my flinch by tugging the coat closer, but Krogan's smile fell. I don't know why but I felt a little like I had just kicked someone's puppy.

"Thanks for saving me," I said, trying to make up for my reaction.

"Why dumb humans play in storms?" He shook his head at me before shuffling over to grab some branches from a pile of wood. He tossed them on the fire and flames burst up, sending me backward. Krogan let out a booming laugh. Before I could find my bearings, I was scooped up in big, furry arms. He was still wet from our fall into the hot springs but he radiated heat. I couldn't help but snuggle into the warmth of his wide chest.

Krogan sat on the rock he'd originally placed me on, settling me into his lap and wrapping his arms around me in a way that told me I wasn't going anywhere. My heart kicked up and I forced myself to remain calm.

So far, he'd done nothing to threaten me. He'd gotten me out of the woods. He'd saved me from drowning in the hot springs and given me a coat to stay warm. I didn't know what time it was, my watch was dead. I had a feeling hours had passed since I'd knocked myself out in the woods and he could have hurt me if he'd wanted to.

Honestly, Krogan seemed like a giant puppy. He'd been silly and funny at the hot springs. He was bossy, but it didn't feel threatening, even when he'd growled at me. I was safe. I had to believe that.

"I didn't mean to be out in the storm," I admitted. "It wasn't supposed to start until later. And I got lost on my way back down the mountain."

"Alone, not safe." His look was reproving. His tone was long-suffering, as though he'd had the conversations many times before.

"I know. I hadn't started off alone, you know. I just... Anyway, thank you." My eyes wandered to the pile of backpacks and hiking equipment in the corner of the cave. Who had they belonged to? What had happened to them?

We sat in silence for a long while, and slowly my body stopped shaking. Between the fire to one side and Krogan to the other, my body warmed. As it did, my brain started to fuzz out. I was physically and mentally exhausted and it was a struggle to stay awake.

My head lolled to the side to settle on Krogan's soft shoulder. The slow and steady movements on his breaths and the thrum of his heart against my ear lulled me into sleep.

Chapter Six

Was it possible for snoring to cause an avalanche? I wasn't sure, but the sounds coming from Krogan made me think I was going to find out. The snoring had woken me from a dead sleep when it started. I'd nearly jumped out of my skin, only the tight grip of the yeti's arms had kept me in place.

We were laying in the bed of furs I'd first woken up in. Krogan was spooned behind me with his arms wrapped tightly around me, much like a small child hugging their favorite toy to sleep. My hair kept blowing over my face as his breath huffed out with each shaking snore.

A rational part of me kept waiting for the panic to sink in. I was being physically restrained by an eight foot tall monster who could easily snap me in half if he wanted to. But honestly? It was comfortable laying there in the bed of furs, wrapped up against the furnace of Krogan's body. He'd had dozens of chances to hurt me if that was what he wanted to do, and he hadn't.

I shifted and Krogan cuddled closer, his body

wrapping tighter around me. His legs curled up behind mine and his front pressed all along my back and oh. Oh!

Okay, apparently snow monsters got hard in their sleep just like your average man. Except there was nothing average about the cock that was pressing against the curve of my ass and poking at the back of my thighs.

My pants were still drying by the fire, which left me in nothing but my thermal long-sleeve shirt and underwear. His cock was hot against my skin, a brand of thick flesh. A part of me was curious about what a yeti's cock looked like. Good sense told me to just lay still and not get myself into trouble with that line of thinking.

It wasn't like he was grinding against me or doing anything to encourage my curiosity. He was asleep. With a hard on. It happened. It was nothing to make a big deal out of. ·

Except, it kind of felt like a big deal. A really big deal.

Krogan shifted on a snort, his top leg moving forward to rest over mine. The movement pushed his cock tighter against me. I couldn't help but squirm against the hard intrusion between my legs. I tilted my hips just slightly until the shaft of his cock was pressed against my cunt.

Heat flared through me as I thought about the possibility of that cock inside of me. I hadn't had sex with anyone but Dylan in over two years. His cock was about average and he was less than inspired at best. He was the type that thought reverse cowgirl was kinky. We'd gotten along well outside of the bedroom and seemed to want the same things out of life, so it had been enough to sacrifice excitement in the bedroom in favor of a solid life together outside of it.

Now, with Krogan's giant cock between my legs, I couldn't stop imagining what it would be like to have something so large inside of me. I couldn't imagine sex with him would be calm or polite. I wiggled, adjusting my position to where his cock was pressed more firmly against me.

The snoring stopped on a groan. I flushed as Krogan's arms tightened around me, hauling me even closer to his chest. His hips thrust forward, sliding that cock along my seam and making me gasp. The arm under my head curved down until his large hand was cupping my breast, kneading the mound of soft, sensitive flesh.

What the fuck was I doing? It was insane. There was no way I was about to fuck a snow beast less than twenty-four hours after I broke up with my boyfriend.

My body didn't appear to be paying attention to the sane part of my brain, though. As Krogan continued his slow grind against me, with his cock trapped between my legs, I couldn't stop myself from grinding back against him. My pussy was wet with wanting. I could feel it seeping out of me and making my panties go damp.

Krogan mumbled something into my hair, his hand tightening around my breast as his thrusts became harder, more forceful, and demanding. I was out of my mind. That was the only excuse I had for what was happening.

Suddenly, Krogan pulled away from me. I whined, turning to face him. The cave was dim with the barest of light coming from the banked coal of the fire. His face was drawn in harsh lines as he stared down at me. The icy blue gaze should have chilled me. It only served to fan the flames higher as he looked me over. His blunt nose flared as he took a deep breath and then he was on me again.

He flopped down on top of me, burying his face in my neck before sliding down my body, sniffing me.

"What smell?" He growled, burying his face into my chest. I stiffened.

"Look, I hiked a damn mountain and haven't showered. It's not like I brought deodorant with me!" I knew I didn't smell daisy fresh, but I hadn't thought I was that bad.

"Smell good." His face slid lower until he nuzzled into my belly before moving to settle with his face between my legs. "Smell like...smell good."

Before I could think to object or decide if it was what I even wanted, Krogan yanked my underwear to the side and buried his face against my cunt. He wasn't licking, just rubbing his furry face against the soft, wet flesh. It felt like he was trying to drown himself in my scent. It should have been ridiculous or a turn off, but for some insane reason it just amped up my arousal.

His fur was soft. It tickled my pussy and thighs and the rounded curve of my belly. His breath was scorching hot. The blunt arch of his nose nudged against my clit and made me gasp. Krogan's eyes flew open and met mine. I'm not sure what he saw on my face, but it was enough to assure him not to quit.

This time, his tongue swept out. It was long

and firm as it moved from hole to clit. Over and over, he licked the same path, two broad fingers holding the gusset of my panties to the side. The grip helped to keep my leg spread wide.

I squirmed under his tongue. I needed more. I needed my clit sucked. I needed something inside of me. My pussy clenched on nothing and my hips arched to get more friction. But he wouldn't give it to me.

Liquid seeped from my core, adding to the hot saliva making a mess of my cunt. This time, when Krogan's tongue moved to my hole, he froze. He growled. And then he was on me like an animal possessed. His tongue stopped the steady swipes and dove deep into my needy vagina. It was broader and longer than any man's tongue and dove deep – searching, seeking, probing. It brushed against my magic spot and I jerked, arching my hips up for more.

That was all it took. The tip of his tongue pressed against the spot over and over again until I was a moaning and panting mess. My hands fisted in his fur as I held him to me, begging him for more, even as my cunt clenched around his tongue.

The sound of tearing fabric ripped through the air and the pressure of my panties tugging against my thigh and ass disappeared. I was too far gone to care. I just opened my legs further to adjust the angle to show Krogan exactly where I wanted him. He growled into my pussy and I was gone.

I sailed over the edge into orgasm. My abs clenched, drawing me up into a crunch as my entire body shook. I wrapped myself around his head as he continued to devour me. He drove me up, up, up again and again until I was sobbing for him to stop. It was too much. The pleasure was too much.

Krogan finally heeded the tugs of his fur and removed his mouth from me. His eyes practically glowed in the dim light of the fire's embers. His hips ground into the pile of furs and a low, keening noise came from his throat. I was completely boneless as I flopped back, unable to hold myself up a moment longer.

"Hay-lee. Mate." Krogan prowled up my body. He paused to press his soaked lips to mine before moving higher until he could press his cock against my wet slit. The slide of the hard flesh against my overstimulated flesh made me shudder.

"Whoa there, big guy." I wiggled up the furs until we were face to face again. He had to be nearly eight feet to my five-five, which meant with our pelvises aligned I was stuck with my face in his chest.

"Hay-lee. Mate." His hips were back to grinding against the bed. Which wouldn't have been so bad, but he was now pressed between my legs and the movement had his belly pressing in a slow grind against my spread pussy. Every nerve ending felt like it was exposed. The sensation was almost overwhelming. Almost.

"There will be no mating with Haley." I said. I wished my voice had been more firm and less breathy. "This is insane."

"Hay-lee." He ground down, his voice a growl of arousal. "Mine. Mate."

"Okay, there is so much wrong with this. So, so much." I buried my hands in the fur of his arms and anchored myself in place as he continued driving me out of my mind with the slow grind. "Fuck. No. We cannot mate. No mate."

"Mine." He growled. And fuck, that growl moved through me. I was as feminist as they come, I'd spent my entire life being strong and independent. I prided myself on never needing anyone, but there was something about that growled claim that shot through my body to my core. "My mate. Mine."

"You can't just claim me as yours, you know. It doesn't work that way." It probably would have been more convincing of an argument if I hadn't been rolling my hips along his torso.

Fuck! He was driving me out of my mind and I was starting to forget why fucking him was a very bad idea.

"Just did." He grinned down at me and I laughed. A laugh that turned into a moan when the grind of his hips met the roll of mine in a perfect connection that had sparks shooting through me. "Hay-lee mine."

Leathery hands tangled in my hair as his mouth descended on mine. His lips were thin, but his mouth was large and overtook mine entirely. He forced his tongue into my mouth and I could taste myself as he kissed me. He gave a little side to side wiggle as he burrowed down against my body and then his hips started little thrusts into the bed. He was panting and growling and my hands were clinging into the fur of his shoulders as I struggled between dueling urges to push him away or drag him closer.

Little whines escaped my throat as I moved against him. His fur a soft tickle over the hard surface of his belly. The hands tangled in my hair pulled just hard enough to add a spark of pain to the overwhelming feeling of the moment. Cold air pressed against the outside of my legs, my body was covered in a sheen of sweat from pleasure and the heat of Krogan's body against mine.

He let out a low growl before pulling away from my mouth and pushed up to his knees. Before I could even think, he pulled me down the bedding until my legs were wrapped around his hips and his hands gripped my thighs. He let go just long enough to angle his cock to line up with my pussy and then he thrust into me.

His cock was huge. A solid ten inches of deep purple flesh jutting out from the white of his fur-covered body. The head was so broad the second it penetrated me, my body clamped down on it and prevented him from moving forward. Despite the many, many orgasms from before and the fact my thighs and his belly were soaked with my fluids, I was nowhere near ready to take something so big.

He growled and pushed forward, forcing himself inside of me. It burned, the stretch so intense and unlike anything I'd ever felt before. I couldn't take my eyes away from where his head was buried inside of me. My pussy was stretched obscenely around him. It was amazing he didn't split me in half with the way he spread me.

I'd expected him to keep thrusting and pushing his way inside of me. Instead, he slowed his forward movement and withdrew to the very tip of his cock before driving in again. I screamed and arched as my body opened for him a little more. Tiny pulses of his hips had him sliding deeper. I dropped my hand to my cunt to rub circles on my clit as he worked himself deep inside of me.

I was impossibly full. There was no way I could take all of him. I sobbed and whined and squirmed. He kept his grip on my thighs and forced me open as he moved deeper and deeper. It was unlike anything I'd ever felt before, more than I could possibly describe. Finally, finally, he was seated all the way inside of me. The tip of his cock pressed almost painfully against my cervix, every movement was almost too much to bear.

"Mine." He growled again. He wrapped a hand around my throat before moving it down my body to where we were connected. He patted my pussy like it'd done a good job before gripping my thigh again. He pressed my thighs impossibly wider.

And then he started to move.

It was slow and stuttering at first as he slid his cock in and out of me. Out a few inches before sliding slowly back in. To the tip before sliding deep. Short thrusts, long thrusts. There was no rhyme or reason to his movements. Still, his cock slid over my g-spot with every thrust and it was enough to have me winding tighter toward orgasm. It wasn't enough to get me there.

I was gripping the furs beneath me for dear life as I tried to thrust against him. The way he was holding me open and down didn't give me any leverage and left me entirely at his mercy. And then suddenly it was like the dam broke and he was moving inside of me in hard, fast thrusts that slid over my g-spot to slam into my cervix and the mix of pleasure and pain was so intense it sent me careening into orgasm.

My eyes rolled back into my head and I screamed my pleasure into the cave. Krogan was grunting with every thrust, but he didn't slow down as I clamped around him. He just kept moving inside of me, his grip on my thighs bruising as he took his pleasure from my body.

The next wave of orgasm had me gasping for air as it washed over me. I'd lost count of the number of times I'd come since we woke up, and every muscle in my body ached and felt like liquid. My heels scrambled against his hips as he kept the brutal, punishing pace.

"Mine." The growl was a claim that shot straight through me. "Mate."

He came on a roar. I could feel him pulsing inside of me, the heat of his cum as he spurted against my cervix and painted my pussy with it. I was on the pill, and had been for years. A stray voice in the back of my mind wondered if it worked against monster sperm. It felt impossible that he could come so hard and so much, fill me so full, and I walk away unscathed.

He pulled from my body, and his absence was like an ache. He collapsed onto his side and cuddled me close to him, wrapping his body around me.

"Mine," he muttered into my hair as his breath slowed from panting gasps to the steady rhythm of sleep.

It was absolutely insane, but a part of me wished it could be true.

Chapter Seven

"What happened to the other humans? The ones whose stuff is in the corner?" I asked as we lay on the bed of furs. Krogan had gotten up long enough to stoke the fire and bring me my pack so I could dig out a couple of protein bars to keep from passing out. We were snuggled together with my head resting on his furry shoulder and my bare leg draped over his upper legs. It was warm and comfortable in the bed. And, while his hand was curved around my ass and hip, there was nothing sexual about the moment.

Still, I needed to know what happened to the people who left their things behind. I knew Krogan hadn't hurt them. I wondered if they ever made it off of the mountain. If they ever came back.

"Gone." The word was a sigh that gave nothing away.

"I know that. Where did they go?" I angled my head to look up at his face, but it gave nothing away. He lay there with his eyes closed and an empty expression.

"Back." He shrugged a little with the shoulder I wasn't lying on. "Left. Never came back."

"They just left their things?" Good hiking equipment wasn't cheap and I could recognize some good supplies in the pile.

"For Krogan." He sighed, a large sound that blew my hair back. "Krogan no need stuff."

I thought about that. About the things in my pack that could make it easier to live in the mountains. The flashlights that would eventually die, the phone without any reception. I supposed the water bottles would be helpful, but he clearly didn't need them. I thought about all of the people who had come before me and then left Krogan there in his cave.

I wondered if he'd claimed any of the others. If he'd taken them as his mate, only to be abandoned. There was so much unsettled about his claim on me, so much I didn't want to look too closely at or examine.

There was no way I could stay in the mountains living in the cave. It wasn't an option. The fact I was willing to kill for a cup of coffee after just one day said it all. I was not a nature girl. I did not go camping. I did not have any desire to homestead or live off the grid.

I liked the grid. I liked electricity and the internet and being able to look shit up on my phone or listen to music whenever the urge struck. I liked nights spent in my warm apartment with an e-reader and a glass of wine. There was not a single part of me that had any desire to live in a cave in the mountains.

Except, for the part of me that wanted to keep

Krogan. That wanted to say fuck reality and disappear with him. The part that loved being snuggled up to him in the warmth of the fire and hearing nothing but the beat of his heart and his soft breaths. The part that wanted to go back to the hot springs and bathe away the sweat of the morning and work up another in the water.

"What about family?" I asked. I would feel less terrible about leaving him if he had someone, anyone, else. "You didn't spring fully grown from nowhere, did you?"

"Gone. All gone. Dead. Left. Krogan the only one who stay." His voice was so sad, lost. It broke my heart to hear him.

"Why did they leave?"

"Yeti hide from humans. Humans harm us. Too many on mountain bad." He shook his head. "Krogan likes humans. Humans funny and dumb. Sometimes they evil and kill. Killed parents. Brothers left. Krogan stay."

There was a moment of silence. I wanted so badly to fill it, but I couldn't think of anything to say. He really was all alone up there and one way or another I would be leaving him soon too.

"Hay-lee family?" At first, I thought he was asking me to be his family. Maybe he was asking about mine since I'd asked about his? Neither question was easy, but I could at least answer the one.

"It's complicated. My parents are serial monogamists with short attention spans." I shifted to sit up, wanting a little distance. "They love falling in love but they hate the work of building a relationship. So they get divorced and move on, no matter who gets hurt in the process."

Krogan also sat up. He cupped my face in his hand, his fingers tunneling into my messy hair. "Hay-lee hurt?"

"Sometimes. Not so much anymore. I stopped getting invested. I have a couple of sisters and a brother. A bunch of people I used to be related to but aren't anymore. Some of them are friends now, I guess."

My half-sister Emma would be looking for me by now. Jessa and Sam, from my father's third marriage and my mother's second, respectively, would notice I was gone after a few days, I was sure. My parents and my younger half siblings probably wouldn't even notice until I didn't show up for Christmas. It was a sad realization.

"Krogan Hay-lee family?" His icy blue eyes were intense on mine and there was a tug in my chest that wanted to say yes. But I couldn't keep him.

"My friend." I said. I put my hand over his where it rested on my face and squeezed. "Krogan Hayley's friend."

His face lit in a wide grin and my heart broke all the more.

Chapter Eight

It was late afternoon, and I was sitting on a rock near the fire when Krogan rushed into the cave. His eyes were wide and a little wild as he looked around the cave. He stopped when he saw me.

I was dressed again in my pants and socks, the coat he gave me draped over my shoulders. I'd been watching the fire and thinking about my next move. The snow had stopped and the sun was back out. There was nothing keeping me in that cave anymore. Nothing except for Krogan.

The smart thing would have been to have him give me directions back to the trail and I could work my way down the mountain. I was sure the Rescue Patrol was out looking for me and, as long as I was near the trail, they were sure to find me. It was the smart, reasonable thing to do.

So why was it so hard to even imagine?

"What's wrong?" I asked Krogan as he barreled toward me and scooped me up into a crushing hug. "What's the matter?"

"Humans." He pressed his face into my hair and breathed deeply. "Hay-lee not gone."

With that sentence my heart broke. Because I knew it was time. I had to go. I had to let everyone know I was okay, and that I hadn't died in the snow storm. I had friends and family that would be worried about me. I had to leave.

We'd talked about it, of course. I'd tried to explain to Krogan why I couldn't stay with him in his cave. I'd promised I would come back and visit him. That I wouldn't abandon him like everyone else. He didn't believe me. He'd stormed out of the cave without a backward glance.

But there we were, back in the moment of me leaving. And I wasn't sure he was going to let me go. I wasn't sure I wanted him to.

"Hay-lee stay." He hugged me impossibly tighter. "Hay-lee mine."

"Oh Krogan, I have to go." I pulled away and took his face into my hands, forcing him to look at me. "I'll come back. I'll come back to see you. I won't leave you alone."

With a growl, he dropped me to the ground. He waited only the barest of moments for me to catch my feet before pulling away entirely.

"Fine." His snarl was vicious and harsh. I tried not to flinch, I wasn't scared of him but the anger hurt me all the same. "Go. Leave. Everyone does."

He left, taking the left tunnel toward the hot springs. The one that would take him away from me and my escape.

I couldn't stop the tears from falling as I laced up my boots. My right ankle was still swollen and sore and I winced as I tightened the laces into place.

My face was wet as I traded the too large coat for my own and picked up my pack.

The ache in my chest was huge as I stopped at the entrance to Krogan's cave. I looked down the left tunnel, wishing he would come back so I could say a proper goodbye. So I could promise again that I would come back to see him, that I wouldn't be yet another person to abandon him.

I could hear the voices now coming from the short tunnel to the right. I followed the path to sunlight. The mouth of the cave was hidden behind an outcropping and a large tree. It was a tight fit. I wondered how Krogan made it carrying me.

On the outside, no one would guess there was anything there. It looked just like any other tree growing against an incline. How the hell would I ever find it again?

I could hear the voices coming closer, and I knew I had to act fast. I pulled the pocket knife from my pack and quickly carved K + H into the tree, marking it as ours. Giving me a way to find my way back to him. I checked my phone and was shocked to find a single bar. It was enough. I dropped a pin in the location to mark it and prayed I'd have service when I came back next time to find my way.

After taking a deep breath of frigid air, I squared my shoulders and started toward the direction I'd heard voices coming from. It was time to get rescued.

/ Chapter Nine

"Are you sure you're okay?" Emma asked me for what had to be the millionth time in the last forty-eight hours. I appreciated her concern. It was the main reason I'd come back off the mountain, but I desperately needed some space and the hovering wasn't helping.

It had taken me less than thirty minutes after leaving the cave to find Search and Rescue. They'd insisted on me going to the hospital to get checked out, despite me insisting I was fine. And I was.

Other than a sprained ankle and minor dehydration, I was the picture of physical health. It was my mental health that was the real issue. Everyone assumed it was the trauma of being left overnight in the mountains in a snowstorm. That wasn't it at all. And it wasn't like I could tell them I'd fallen in love with a Yeti who'd rescued me from dying of hypothermia and gave me the best dicking of my life.

Even if they did somehow believe me, it would only put Krogan at risk. I wouldn't do that. I would do anything to keep Krogan safe. Even if it meant letting everyone I knew and loved believe I was suffering from PTSD.

"I'm fine, Emma." I adjusted the blanket over my lap and opened her laptop. I still hadn't been to the apartment I'd shared with Dylan yet to get my own. It was something I would have to deal with sooner rather than later, but I wasn't ready yet. "Go to work. I'll be fine. I'm going to look for a new place to live so I can get out of your hair."

She hesitated for a long moment in the kitchen before nodding and putting her coffee mug on the counter. "If you're sure. I do have that project due on Friday and I'm days behind now."

I tried not to flinch. It hadn't been an accusation, but I still felt guilty. I was the reason she was behind, and it wasn't like I'd ever been in any danger. No, I'd been safe, cared for, and treasured more in the time I was gone than I had been in my life.

Thirty minutes later, Emma was on the way out the door and I was left alone in her small one-bedroom apartment. I opened maps on my phone and looked at the pin I'd dropped in the mountains, wishing I could see the spot. Be there again.

No, I had a plan and work to do before I went back up the mountain. I had to be ready next time I saw Krogan. I owed it to both of us to be ready.

* * *

It took me two months to get everything together. It was the longest, most stressful two months of my life.

Everyone thought I was suffering from PTSD

from my night in the mountains, that I had lost my mind and was acting crazy. And I probably was.

Who in their right mind changed their entire lives based on a single night with someone? So, maybe I wasn't in my right mind. I knew deep down I was making the right decision. Krogan had made me feel more important and special in that single night than I had felt with anyone else in my life before.

Plus, I'd made a promise. One I intended to keep.

There was a warm snap in late January that cleared the snow on the mountain path enough for me to make the climb with the help of walking sticks. It was brutal. The cold air made my lungs ache, and I was out of shape; not having time in the previous months to get to the gym.

Emma had about lost her mind when I'd told her I was going back up the mountain. She'd tried to insist on coming with me, but it was a hike I had to make alone. Maybe one day she'd understand, but for now, Krogan was my secret.

I followed the trails as far as I could until I was parallel with the red pin I'd dropped. My heart raced as I neared it. Exertion was some of it, sure. But fear coursed through me as well.

What if Krogan was gone? Or he didn't want me anymore? What if he rescued some other girl on the mountain who wasn't stupid and never left him?

My hands were clammy in my gloves as I started searching the trees along the stone outcroppings in the area, looking for my tree. The one I'd marked for us. I was running out of time to find it if I wanted to get out of the mountains before nightfall.

And I did.

Oh, I desperately did not want Emma to send another search and rescue team looking for me. The attention from the last "Missing Hiker Found Safe" news stories had just died down. No way I wanted to go through that again. Especially not if I had Krogan with me. And I desperately wanted to have Krogan with me when I left the mountain.

"Krogan," I called softly, hoping he would hear me and make this easier. I didn't want to yell too loud and attract attention if anyone else happened to be up there with me.

I had nearly made it to the tree when a giant white creature threw itself out of a crack in the stone. I yelped and stumbled back, falling onto my butt in the remaining snow.

"Hay-lee!" His grin was side and a little goofy as he raced over to haul me off the ground and into his arms. "Hay-lee back!"

I wrapped my arms around his shoulders, burying my face in the fur around his neck and breathing in the warm, earthy scent. His grip on me was almost too tight as he squeezed me to his body and started walking back to his cave.

Time was running out for me to get off the mountain and I needed to explain my plan to him, but I took the moment for us to just exist together. I felt so safe and warm and cherished as he crushed me to him.

"I can't stay long." He let out a low growl and pulled back to glare down at me. His teeth were bared, but I didn't flinch. Krogan wouldn't hurt me. "I want you to come with me."

"Krogan stay. Krogan's mountain." He pounded the side of his fist along the wall of the cave near the entrance to the cavern he called home. "Hay-lee stay."

He carried me to his cavern and set me on my feet by the pile of furs. His large hands went to my zipper, pulling it down in one swift movement. He tried to shove it off, but I gripped his wrists. As much as I wanted his hands on me, we didn't have the time. Not here. Not now.

"I can't stay here, Krogan. Humans aren't made to live in caves like this." I stroked my hands up his arms to grip his shoulders. "You could come with me."

"Krogan no go to humans home. Not safe. Keep Hay-lee safe here." His arms wrapped around my waist and hauled me up into his arms again. His icy eyes practically glowed in the dim light of the fire.

"Not where humans are. I bought a place for us. For you and me and only us. There's lots of land and we'd be safe there."

It had taken time and some doing. Dylan and I had been looking for a house, but I'd had to reapply for the mortgage without him. The perfect place had practically fallen ynto my lap. It was a small, single bedroom cabin on a small plot of land. It backed up to a national forest which would give Krogan lots of room to roam. The road up was practically non-existent in bad weather, but I worked from home and would learn to adjust. Having Krogan there would be enough.

I knew I was asking a lot of him. That he could decide not to come with me and I'd be stuck with a remote cabin where I'd likely die alone. It was worth the risk. As insane as it was to fall in love with someone after one day, I was and there was no denying it.

"Please Krogan, come with me. Be with me. Let me keep you." His face was dark and my heart sank. He was going to say no. Of course he was. I was asking so much.

"Hey-lee mine? Hay-lee mate?" I nodded rapidly.

"Yes. I'm yours. All yours."

Six Months Later

My entire body relaxed when I pulled my SUV into the driveway and my little wood cabin came into view. The roses the previous owner planted were a cheery pop of color under the front windows on either side of the path. Everywhere I looked, things were green and coming back to life after the long winter.

I'd been ready to lose my mind when we'd had the unexpected snow storm in early May that kept us trapped on the mountain for a solid five days. There was apparently a learning curve to survival prepping, and I'd failed at it. Terribly.

Thankfully for all of the issues we'd had, Krogan hadn't minded. Used to surviving the winter in the woods, he'd helped see us through in a number of ways, including finding small game to cook and building fires when the storms took the electricity out. We were a team. Something I never expected to have.

I parked the SUV and went to open the hatch. I had a meeting in town and then stopped at the store to pick up supplies. We were expecting rain, lots of it, in the next few days. There was a risk of the drive getting washed out.

At first, the disconnect from the modern world had stressed me out. Now I kind of liked that we were so cut off out there. The little cabin in the woods was my oasis, and I could hardly relax whenever I had to leave it. And the giant Yeti that lived within.

Speaking of, where was my Yeti? Normally, he was out the door the moment the car stopped, ready to scoop me up as if I'd been gone weeks, instead of hours.

Curious but not concerned, I carried in the perishables and put them away. I left everything else in the SUV and started down the nearly worn path toward the nature reserve woods behind the cabin.

"Krogan?" I called, stepping into the shade of the trees and meandering between the wide trunks. There were no set paths here, no way to mark the course. I wouldn't go too deep into the woods without Krogan or else I would end up lost. He had an amazing internal GPS while I was likely to get lost the second I could no longer see the house.

"Krogan?" I called again as I reached the furthest point I could go without fear of getting stuck in the woods. "Okay, if you can hear me, I'm home. I'm going to start dinner soon."

I'd hoped the promise of food would have pulled him out of whatever he was doing, but there was no response. I sighed and started back toward the house. Our home.

The concept still made me all warm inside. For a while, I had been so scared that it wouldn't work with Krogan. He'd gotten violently carsick on the ride from his mountain to the house. He'd bolted into the woods the second the car stopped on the turn and hadn't reemerged for two days. I'd been terrified he'd left somehow.

After two days of staring into the woods, my heart was in my throat when he came up to the cabin. He'd taken me into the woods to a cave he found there. It wasn't as large or as nice as the one on his mountain, but he said it would do.

Slowly, though, Krogan had come to enjoy the many modern conveniences I refused to live without. He still preferred his meat cooked over an open flame rather than in the oven, but he was a big fan of pasta in all forms. I'd introduced him to the magic of hot showers, which he loved. Coffee, which he hated. And TV, which confused him.

Still, a Yeti was a Yeti, and Krogan spent much of his day in the woods while I worked at my computer on the kitchen table. But he somehow always knew when I was wrapping things up and showed up at the door with a wide, toothy grin. So his absence was definitely confusing.

I was nearly out of the woods when large arms wrapped around my middle and hauled me off my feet. I screamed and kicked my feet out before I realized I knew the feel of the body behind me.

"Jesus Krogan, you scared the crap out of me!" I gripped the arms wrapped around me and craned my neck until I could glare up into his broad, grinning face. He looked so stupid happy, I couldn't even be mad at him for scaring me.

"Hay-lee home!" He nuzzled his face into my neck and cuddled me closer for a moment before setting me back on my feet. I was barely balanced before I spun back around and launched myself into his arms.

As crazy as it had been to change my entire existence for a creature I'd only known a day, it had been the best decision I'd ever made. Krogan cared about me and for me in a way I could have never imagined.

"Missed you." I muttered, pressing my lips to his. "Where were you?"

"Cave. Come see." He set me to my feet and took my hand, leading me to the cave he'd turned into his man cave. It wasn't terribly far from the house, maybe a forty minute hike. But I definitely hadn't planned on the walk and my skirt and flats, which weren't the best for tromping through the woods. Krogan would have carried me if I'd asked, but then he'd tease me for being a silly human.

Light flickered at the cave's entrance, a sure sign Krogan had lit a fire in there. Curious, I glanced at him, but he just nudged me ahead of him into the cave. I stopped just through the entrance to stare in wonder.

There was a small fire, but it was the rest of the cave that caught and held my attention. There was an actual mattress laying near the fire heaped in pillows and blankets. Early wildflowers were in mason jars scattered everywhere. Camp lights, currently unlit, stood by the doorway. There was a folding chair and a folding loveseat set up near the fire.

"What?" I looked back at Krogan again, loving the grin on his face but wondering how and why he'd done this. "How?"

"Emma help." Emma had shown up unannounced about a month into moving Krogan into our house. She'd taken the fact I was dating a Yeti fairly well. She'd only fainted once, and it hadn't lasted long. Emma adored Krogan, and the feeling was very mutual. "Our secret place. Just for Krogan and Hay-lee."

My hand went to my chest, pressing against the painful beating of my heart. It was so lovely and surprising and just like Krogan. He'd needed a cave, but he'd made it somewhere I would be comfortable too.

"And for cubs?" His expression was sly, his voice hopeful. I choked.

"No. Nope. We've talked about this." I still wasn't convinced I wanted children. And we didn't even know if it was possible to have a Yeti/Human child.

"Try. Now." He was on me in a heartbeat. He scooped me up and threw me over his shoulder on his path to the bed. He dropped me onto the mattress and before I even stopped bouncing, he was on me.

His mouth took mine in a sloppy kiss, all puppy-like enthusiasm. It made me laugh, just like it always did. Nothing about sex with Krogan was neat or polished or tame. Sometimes sex was a near-violent need that held us in a vice-like grip. Other Times it was playful and silly. Krogan wasn't a skilled lover, but he was an enthusiastic one. All of that enthusiasm focused my way was seriously addicting. It was a heady thing, being wanted that way.

Krogan didn't bother to unbutton my blouse. He just grabbed both sides in his big hands and yanked it apart. Buttons popped and flew in all directions as he spread the cloth and bent down to nuzzle and mouth at my breasts.

My laugh broke off on a moan when he sucked hard at one nipple through my lace bra. He stayed there, moving from breasts to breast until I was a panting and writhing mess before moving his head down between my legs. He licked and sucked me through the lace of my panties with his head buried under my skirt.

Over the last few months, he'd learned my body's signals and knew when I was nearly there. He enjoyed making me come over and over again until I was spent and begging him to stop. This time, though, he stopped with me on the edge and prowled up my body. A hard twist in my panties had the sides snapping and the flimsy lace was gone.

"Hay-lee mine." He growled against my mouth before continuing up my body until his cock was poised at my entrance. It didn't matter how many times we had sex, I was never quite prepared enough for the size of him. Our size difference had my face at pectoral level as he gently pushed inside of me.

He rocked into me with short thrusts until he was buried deep inside of me. I wrapped my arms and legs around him, holding him close as he started to move with little grunts. I gasped my pleasure into his chest. It didn't take long until the edge of pleasure I'd been riding came back and washed over me again.

The second my pussy started to clench around his shaft, he was gone. He thrust as deep as he could go and, with the tip of his penis pressed against my cervix, he emptied himself inside of me.

Krogan rolled us until he laid on his back on the bed before pulling me off his cock and up to cuddle my head on his shoulder. His large arms wrapped around me as I snuggled into his soft, warm body.

"Hay-lee mate." Krogan said, kissing my head.

"Krogan mate," I whispered back. "But I'm still not having cubs."

"We see." Krogan said, hugging me tight. And okay, I had no clue what the future would bring. But with Krogan, anything was possible.

About the Author

Sabrina Cross (she/her) is a neurospicy 80's baby from the middle of nowhere Michigan, where she still lives with her cat. She came into her monster romance era early when she fell in love with Beast from the 1997's X-Men animated series. After discovering sentient object romance in early 2023, Sabrina decided to embrace what she calls her 'Hold My Beer' style of writing and gave into the lifelong dream of being an author. When not writing weird monster/sentient object smut, Sabrina can be found hanging out on social media (@authorsabrinacross), reading, or hoarding office supplies.

Also by Sabrina Cross

Yarn & Monsters Series

A True Love Spell Gone Wrong...

When four friends perform a true love spell, things go terribly wrong. Now they're locked into a deal with the devil and have only a year to find love and happiness or their souls are destined to face the flames. Armed with a demon guardian; Clover, Jasmine, Fern, and Violet are determined to beat the devil and save themselves. Except, this curse might be the best thing that's ever happened to them.

Corny: A F/F Candy Corn Romance

A True Love Spell Gone Wrong...

A Demon Fairy Godmother?

Her very soul on the line. Can Clover still find true love or is she destined to face the flames alone?

Snuggle: A M/F Demon Teddy Bear Romance

A True Love Spell Gone Wrong...

Jasmine is too busy to go to Hell and she's definitely too busy for demon antics. But when her demon "Fairy Godmother" shows up, everything is on the line. Does she have what it takes to get out of the Devil's bargain or is she doomed to face the flames?

Tangled: A M/F Friends-To-Lovers Sentient Object Romance

A True Love Spell Gone Wrong...

Fern is going to Hell. Not metaphorical Hell but actual,

physical Hell. But there's one thing she needs to do before she goes. An item she desperately needs to scratch off the bucket list. And she's hoping the demon sent to guard her will be willing to help her out.

Knotted: A M/F Demon Werewolf Romance

A True Love Spell Gone Wrong...

Violet was no witch but that didn't stop her from trying to use magic to find love. When the spell backfired and left her and her friends bound in a deal with the devil, Violet vowed to find a solution. Now, with less than two months until the deal comes due and zero leads, she's facing the fire. The fire comes early in the form of a great black beast in her bed. Does Violet find the love she's been looking for or does Hell claim her soul?

Light Me Up

He was the first man to ever turn me on. When he flipped my switch and lit me up that first time, I knew he was it for me. There would never be another.

Pounded by the Pommel Horse

Elena loves being on top. When the elite gymnast is challenged to defeat her gym rival on the pommel horse, she's up for the task. But is she up for the ride when the pommel horse shapeshifts into a man? A very, very naked Man?

Christmas with the Monster

He's Got a Package for Her... Devynn expected her first holiday without her kids to be difficult. But nothing could have prepared her for what she found under the tree just after midnight.With the help of his magic sack, the furry, green giant promises Devynn all kinds of pleasure. But would one night with the Christmas monster ever be enough?

Sentient Pen15 from Outer Space

Liam had spent a lot of his childhood obsessed with the legends of the local mines. The abandoned tunnels underground had driven dozens of workers insane and young Liam was desperate to get to the bottom of it. But he found more than he bargained for down there.

Infected by parasitic space mold, Liam has held himself away from relationships for years. When things spark between him and the girl next door, he has no choice but to reveal the truth: his manly appendage is also the bane of his existence.

The Cursed Matchmaker Series

The Glory Whole Package

Never Piss Off a Witch.

It is a hard-learned lesson and one I may never complete. The endless boredom of my curse is only broken by analyzing the people who use me.

Today I break my silence for the first time and while it might lead to a Happily Ever After, it will never be mine. Not until I've paid for my crimes and earned the forgiveness of the only person I've ever loved.

The Glory Whole Experiment

Some curses aren't meant to be broken...

And there's no escaping mine. For two years I've been trapped in the dark, being used, remaining silent. But I'm a man on the edge. When another couple enters my booth, something changes. I'm not able to keep silent anymore. Not this time.

Is this a new facet of my curse or is the magic fading?

The Glory Whole Experiment is a deeply unserious story about a man cursed to be a glory hole. It is intended for audiences 18+. Please see author notes at the beginning of the book or on my website for further details.

Retro Whimsy Series

Getting Railed

"Welcome to Retro Whimsy!"

I hadn't planned on buying anything when entering the new vintage store during my lunch break but somehow found myself leaving with a toy train set.

What could have been written off as an impulse purchase became so much more when those trains come to life.

Now I'm stuck dealing with the consequences of a god curse and deciding if I have what it takes to help break it.